Selected Works

Selected Works

By

Stephen Mead

ISBN
978-0-6151-4160-2

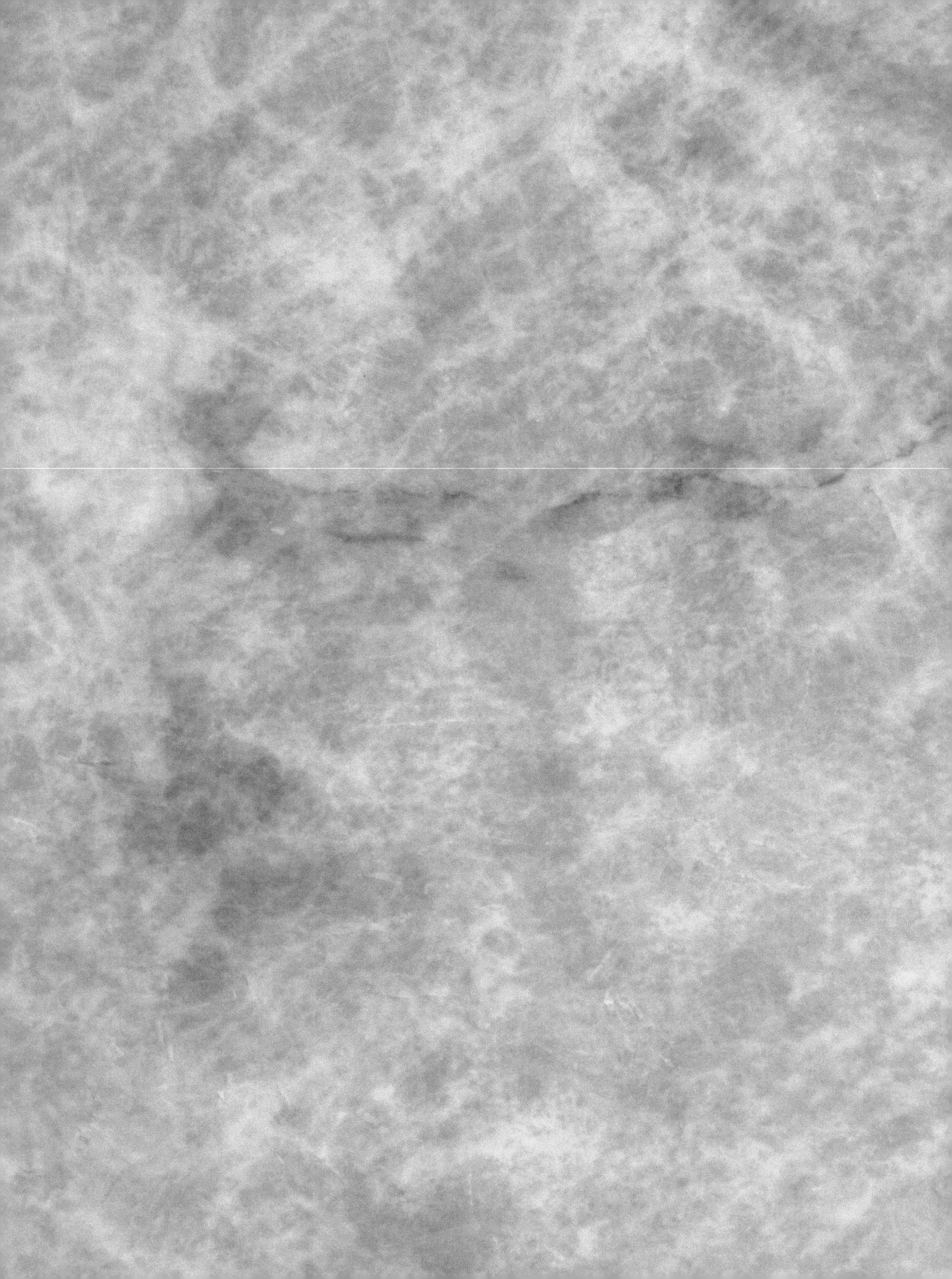

"Body as Landscape"
poetry & art by Stephen Mead

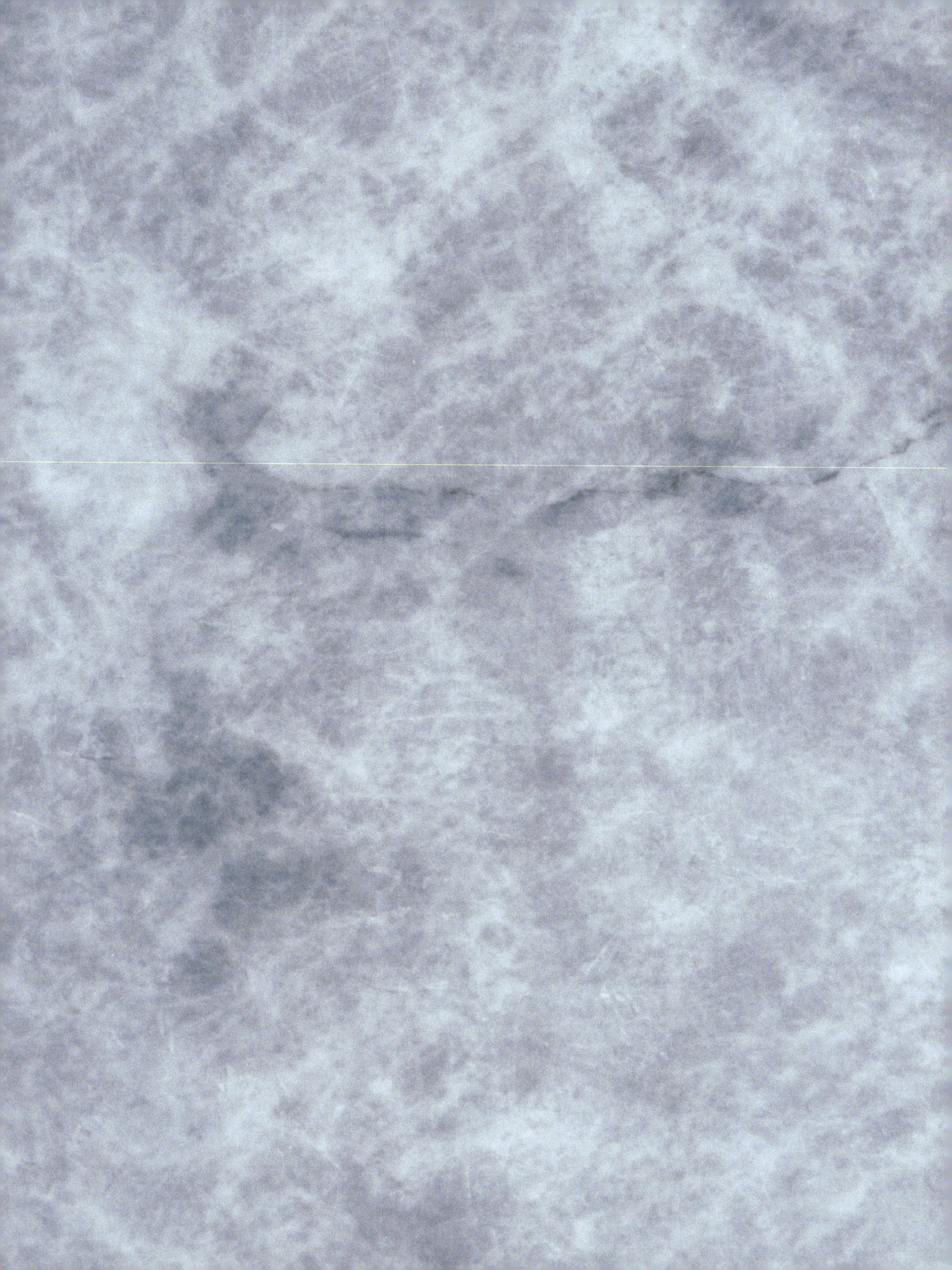

Hands on feet,
a respite this,
to crouch here observant
on golden shores,
these veins, rivers,
over the footholds
of bones
pulsing to your slumber.
They almost purr.

The legs, an arch,
to climb such a slope
with fingers
as a wind ripple,
with tongue,
a caress;
    & the exploration
is sure
as any earthly plateau
heavens hold
the horizon of.
    Let us go on.

4

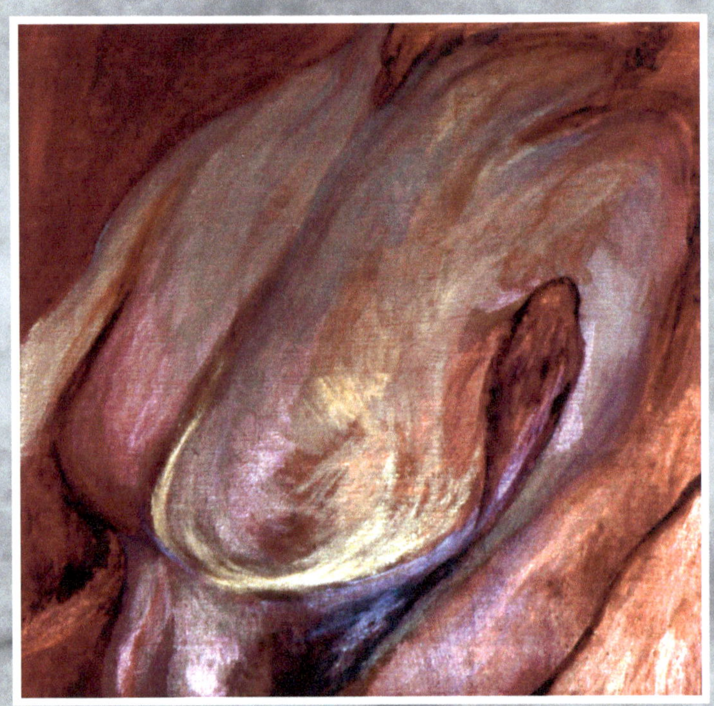

Breasts, dearest,
they are orbs
of the horn,
cornucopia firm,
with milk as honey,
the fertile fruit
in store
tender as a warrior
in Amazon strength
cradling scars.

6

"Yonder", the stretch sighs,
torso of holiness,
the sacred ribs,
a hull of breath
flickering with spirit life
candle warmest
towards the belly
which yeilds
loin ripe
between hips,
    & which of us afloat,
which of us gondolier?

8

Lover, the copper canyon's birth
is a field of bronze.
Are these yours'
or mine,
these shimmers waving
in a valley of hope
to rise forth from
and find summits
summoning: "Sail more!"

10

Lover, up close
the world turns
into Gulliver,
    & are we the lilliputians
or giants equal?
    I do not know
any more knowledge
than these rolling folds,
these gentle flats.
    Teacher, be compass,
be map, our sojourn
a bas relief
of pleasures tactile.

Face away,
what a shelter, the back,
what messages
in the shoulders.
They are ensigns
of invitations.
Commisar, I listen,
hear what you receive.

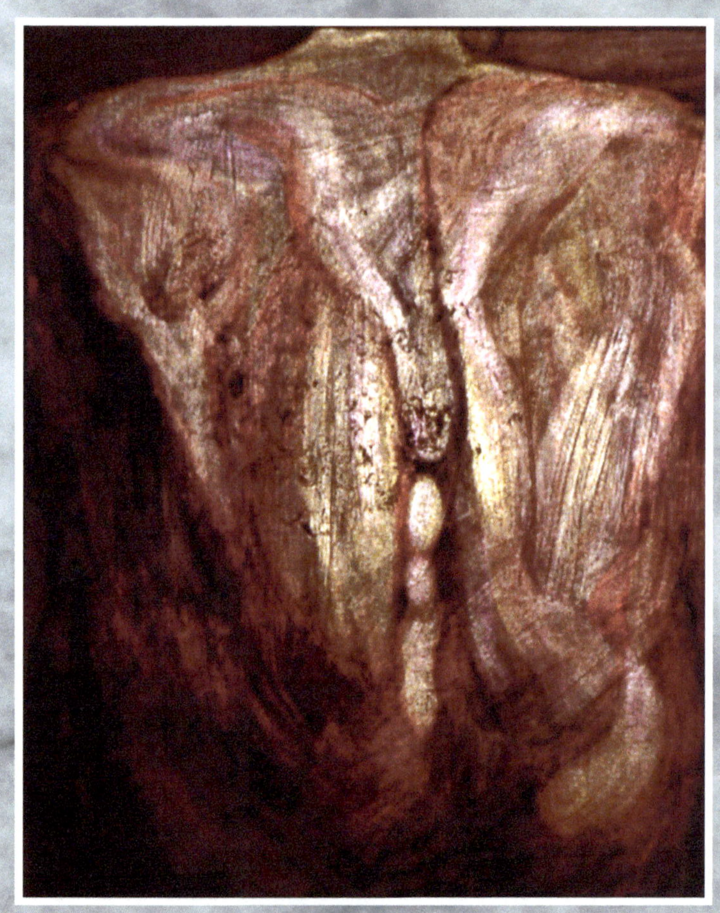

Stand up, lovely laborer,

such tides

your curves sweep

ocean sure as a port

vessel blessed

by its very nature

to center the frame

as a trunk

the moon rushes up

for a tree of arms.

16

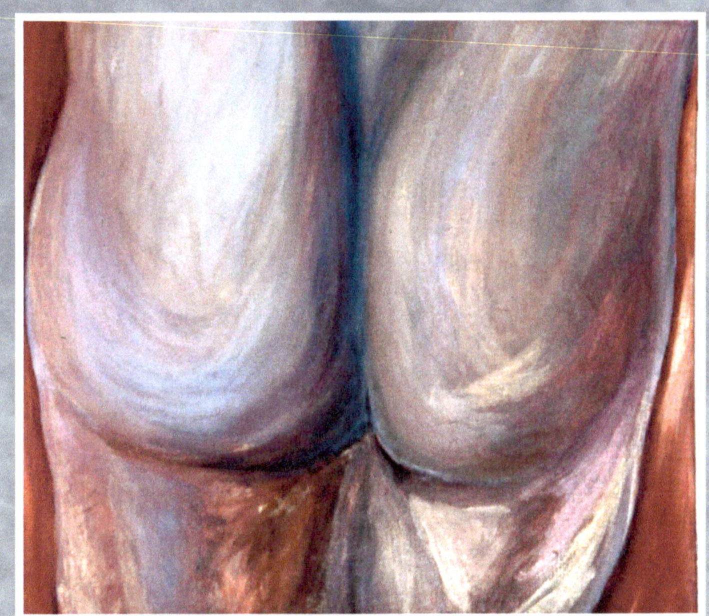

Turn around,

a ceremonious throne,

honor-sitting,

belly-wide, regal,

a dream of the sun

real as a spear,

or an oar

with which to stroke

waters, navigate the course.

18

Oh lover,
this is the whole picture,
from mountains,
alps of light,
to the shadows
red with heat,
our efforts, flames...
sensuous with glory,
a prostration of religion,
this body, this skin,
all our soul has,
given unto,
given as treasure.

20

"WASHING THE BODY"
POEM & ARTWORK BY STEPHEN MEAD

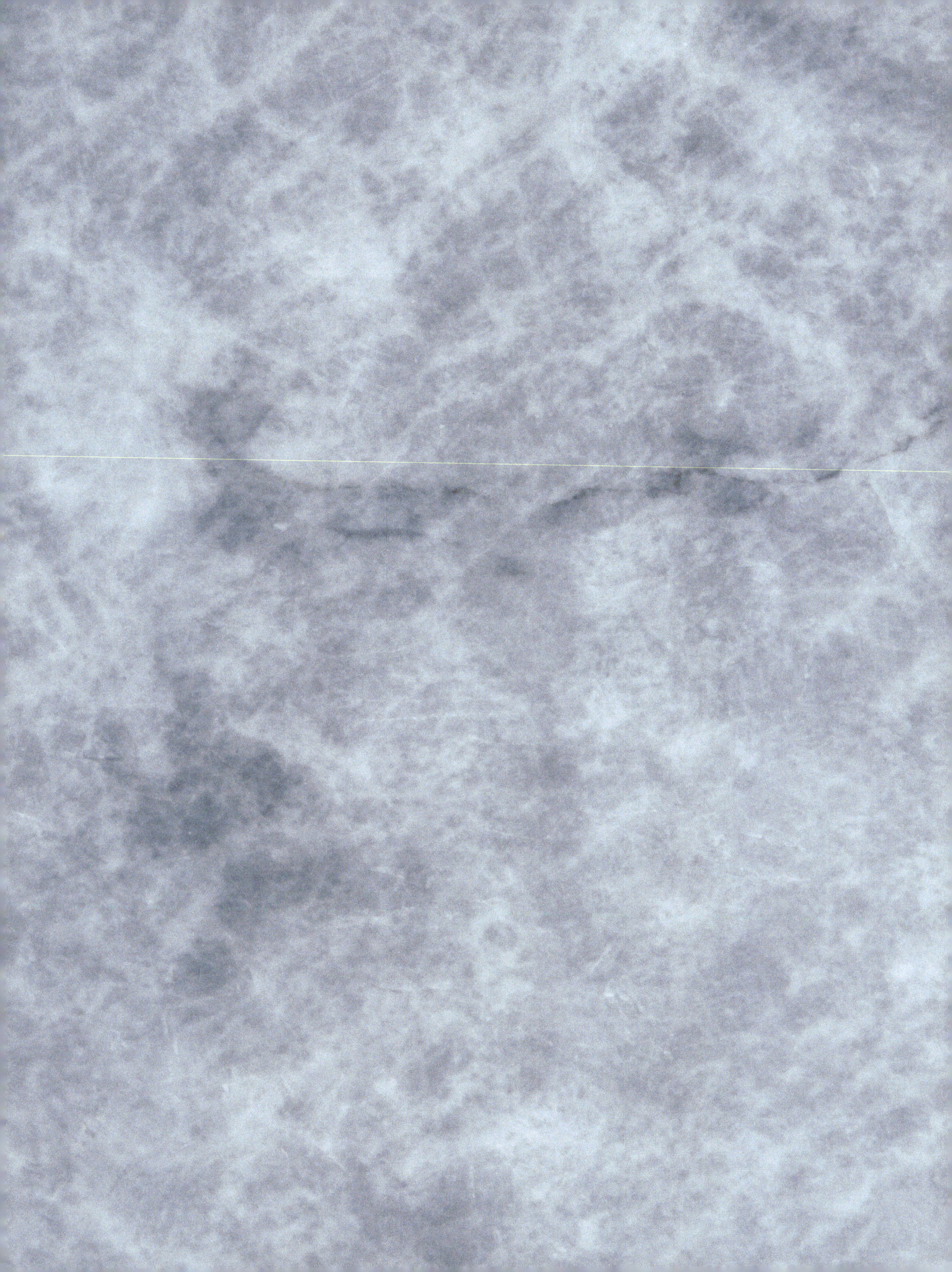

LOTUS OPENS,
PETALS MAGENTA
IN A BLOSSOM OF BLUE,
THE PALM OF A SAINT
FIST-CURLED
YET DELICATE,
INTRICATE OVER
THE BOWL, HALO-GOLDEN

SPONGE COME FORTH
HOLY AS A TESTAMENT,
THE WEATHERED HANDS
WHICH GIVE OATH,
SCRIPTURES IN THEMSELVES
OF PARCHMENT & LEATHER
BEHELD BY A ROBE
SORROW THICK
AS FAITH

PG 4

SPONGE CHRIST,
WE ANOINT YOU,
WHATEVER MODERN DAY SOUL
YOUR SKIN CHRISTENS
& THE SPONGE, A HOST
FOR THE INNOCENCE
WITHOUT MARTYRDOM
SAVE THE HUMANITY
IN BEING A TRIPTYCH
OF VISION, BONE, BLOOD

SPONGE CHRIST,
YOUR EYES ARE KNOWING
WITHOUT BEING TERRIBLE,
GHOST-LIKE OR PALE.
NO, THE TRANSCENDENT GAZE
BEAMS GRATEFUL EMPATHY
THROUGH THE TRANSLUCENCE
OF THE SPIRIT
SHINING ITS LOVE
ON RECEPTION
LIKE RAYS
OF A CRADLED CROWN

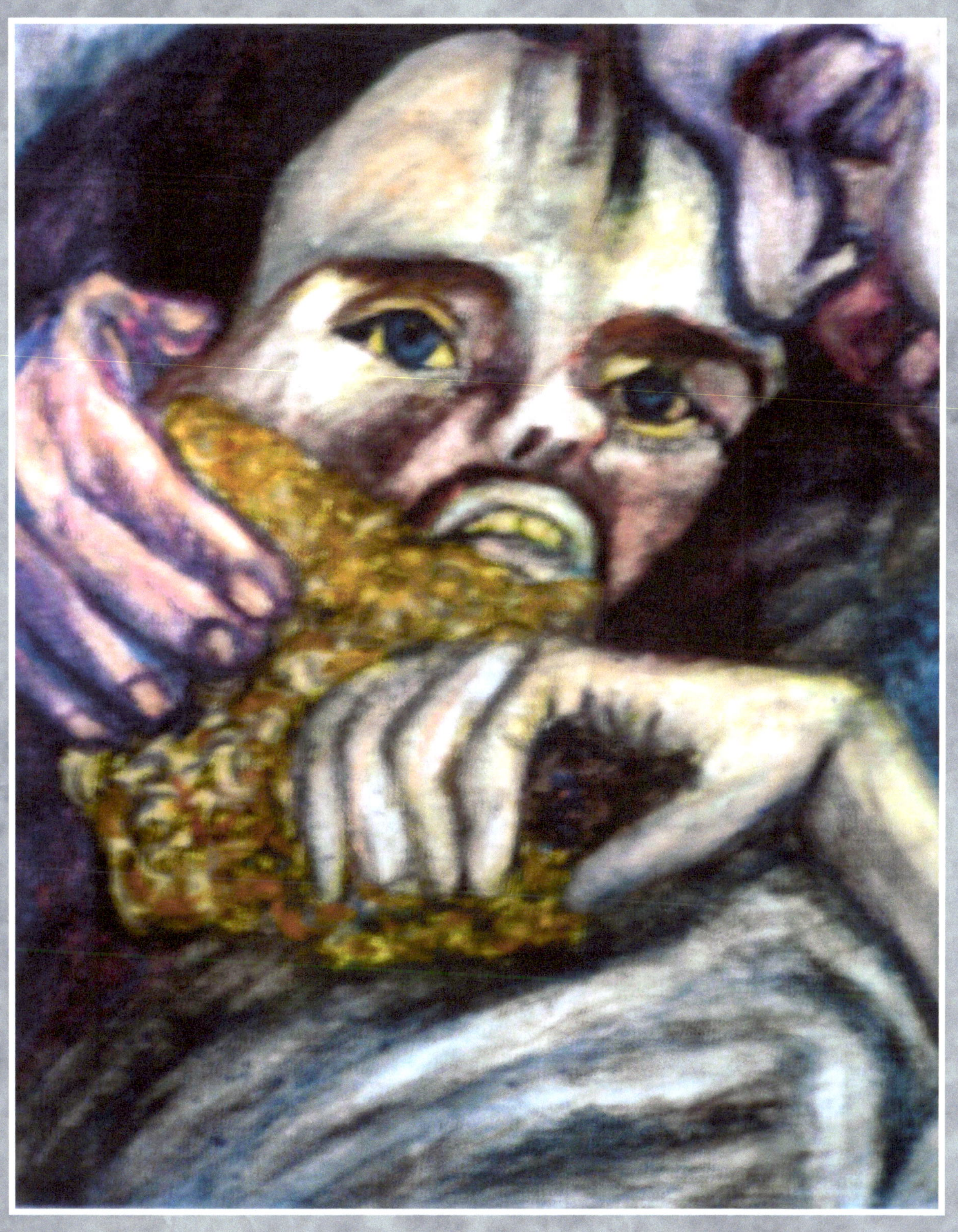

NOW POUR OVER THE HAIR,
RINSE WITH ROSE WATER,
A PEWTER CLEANSING
A PURE PERFUME OF MYRRH
SANCTIFIED BY THE HOLD
OF TOWEL & BASIN,
THE PITCHER'S LIP
CASCADING ITS SPILL,
SILVER-WHITE,
THE VOWS REFLECTING

SUCH IS THE PROMISE
THESE FEET HAVE WALKED,
THE MANNA OF MILES
IN THE MOUNDS
& THE TOES.
SUCH IS THE PROMISE
BLANKETS SWADDLE
& SHEETS SING
IN THE STREAMS OF
ALL OF LIFE SWIRLING

LOVE, WHATEVER DARKNESS
WILL HAVE YOU,
WHATEVER EGGPLANT PURPLE,
WHATEVER ROYAL SILK
IS WOVEN ALSO OF RADIANCE.
EXISTENCE STILL THE PROPHESY
IN ELECTRIC DUST
& PASSING CELLS,
THE STUFF OF METAMORPHOSIS
FIREFLY BRIEF
EXCEPT IN THE HEARTS
YET CHERISHING
THE MEMORIES PRESERVED
BY EMBLAZONED SUMMER

PG 13

HOW THE HEAD REMAINS A VESSEL,
THAT DIGNIFIED KINGDOM,
THE SKULL EGYPTIAN,
AN ONYX ROSE.
THE PETALS OF FACE PLANES
ARE WONDROUS LANDSCAPES,
& ALL IN ALL THE STARS KNOW
THE HORIZONTAL
IS ROUND ETERNALLY

SO COME MY ANGELS,
MY GRACES.
COME MERCIFUL HEAVENS.
LET TENDERNESS WASH US
EACH IN OUR HONOR
HONORING OUR STRUGGLE

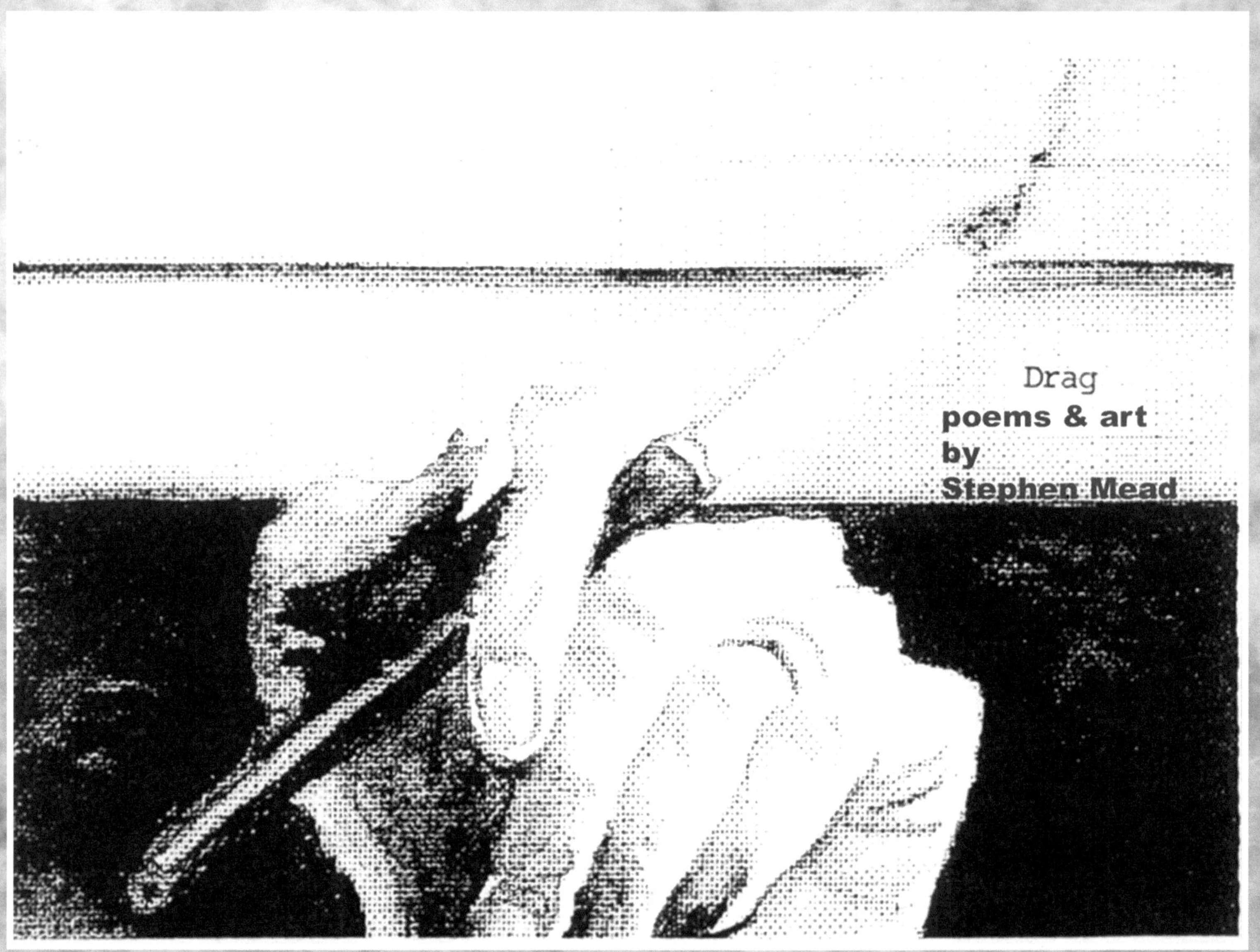
Drag
poems & art
by
Stephen Mead

"It's a drag to want someone so much...and the drag is, I will live without you,
I just don't want to." Syd Straw

"Every day I thank God I can smoke a cigarette
when I'm choking inside. "   Yoko Ono

"What are you takin' for beautie's sake?" Marianne Faithfull

Exhale, smoke wreathed,
The spinning dreams start.
Am I dragon princess
Beneath this smog,
Foggy shifter,
Mysterious chameleon?
As scent you know me,,
Wafting wisps, ash acrid.
Take a whiff.
This mist is diaphanous.
Secrets retreat.
Like pets I shall name them,
Perfume-linger, & be gone.

3

Exhale, smoke wreathed,
The spinning dreams start.
Am I dragon princess
Beneath this smog,
Foggy shifter,
Mysterious chameleon?
As scent you know me,,
Wafting wisps, ash acrid.
Take a whiff.
This mist is diaphanous.
Secrets retreat.
Like pets I shall name them,
Perfume-linger, & be gone.

Tissues, mouth imprinted,
Rouge pots & cold cream
For the kohl
Above the nose
Powdered to a blush
From the copper compact,
The lipstick tasting of tin
Hidden from perspective
Amid the wig stand & boa...
Oh la la la
"I feel pretty"
a West Side Story miniature
in this lens-----
Mirror, mirror, who is fairest
When this land's apocalyptic?
Eyes, the soul's own looking
Glass camera records
The business all the live long day,
But I look through them
Searching only for you
Again & again

Voyager now,
What vanishing has begun?
My hat is a sail,
The face, a masthead,
& clouds a prow
Around adrift schooner shoulders.
I travel this, a heroine Columbus
Discovering myself a new life.
Light my cigarette, would you?
How kind & good.
I should tip the brim
Shadowing my gaze.
I am Bette Davis
Just waiting for the close-up
To focus on you properly.
Then will this toy top
Of a world
Finally stop spinning?

7

Today I will be lovely Greta,
Clear as swedish rivers
With gin neat repose
And a not-so-cold glance,
Aloneness my friend,
A thousand years of it,
And that solitude grand.
Yes, in this stillness
Ye shall know
How this silence listens,
Vigilant, omniscient,
The watcher through
Timelessness,
And I am water, not stone,
Holding music like glass.

Crystal too, dear Marlene,
Long vase statue,
Hair, brow, voice,
Enduring flowers.
"Shut up & kiss,"
Said this Helen herself,
Destroyer of men & not
Androgynous a bit
Even when tuxed,
When evasive Mata Hari
In the house of love,
More loving than loveless,
Spied on, reclusive
Past her legend-----
Youth freckling to
Age spots but
Like a monarch,
Like moths falling in,
Clustered to the inferno,
The wick

Rain on the tongue,
Such bovine innocence,
Such sweetness, girl,
Your delectable skin
Edible as buttermilk bread.
Was Norma Jean slaughtered
In you like a lamb
For the Hollywood homes,
Each a fled orphanage?
Dead or alive
Your glamorous myth lives
With new rumors yet
To your life.
Still your eyes tell the truth,
Photographed once
On a Sunday
Leaning from a window
On the set.
In that moment
You were at ease,
With the incandescent
Vulnerability, the intelligence
 Womanly,
 warm & soft
As your terry cloth robe,
as the nakedness it scarcely
Knew how to protect

Wisecracking
Mae saunters
Come up, see
 entendres, double,
Hear high jinks,
Note the circus
Bump & grind
Like a caboose loose
On curvaceous
Tracks.
Here is slapstick.
Here is wit
Rambunctious
As skits of vaudeville
Juggling W.C. &
Groucho &
Durante-ish
Buster Keaton.
She has it all baby,
With a flutter & bat,
A flip & a roll,
Blonde bombshell
Slick & sly.
Sex, the joke.
Sex, the independence.
You better, you ought to,
Believe it kid

Star born, born Gumm,
When the rainbow was over
Where in hell was our Judith?
I've seen her in piano bars,
Re-habs, diners,
Belting show tunes
Which stopped any crowd
Like an avalanche.
Heck,
She was just human,
Addicted, addicting,
No stranger to her faults.
Come Judy, here
Are your shades.
Tie this scarf
About your head.
We'll find a park & sit
Close as weathered pigeons,
Drinking coffee, sharing
A giggle.
Sure, we will be confidantes
Whispering thief thick &
In a moment
All of the gray
Will be over like
a witnessed
Nuremberg.
Judy, where are you?
Clang, clang, clang
Your trolley heart is
Tinsel speed
The reels are flashing
With like celluloid
gas

17

Piaf, sparrow littlest,
The tremulous throat,
The tune of the thrush
With tragic vibrato
Thunderously echoing...
Yes, how resonance lasts,
French vowels like comets
Out of the darkness
 of the Olympia.
So applause lingers
Like arbutus drizzle,
And spotlights tumble,
Scatter tympanic
From crashing waves of sky.
But, la vien, hushed,
In the aftermath
Opens up the rose
With "if you love me,
Really love me, then
Let it happen",
And nothing is lost

19

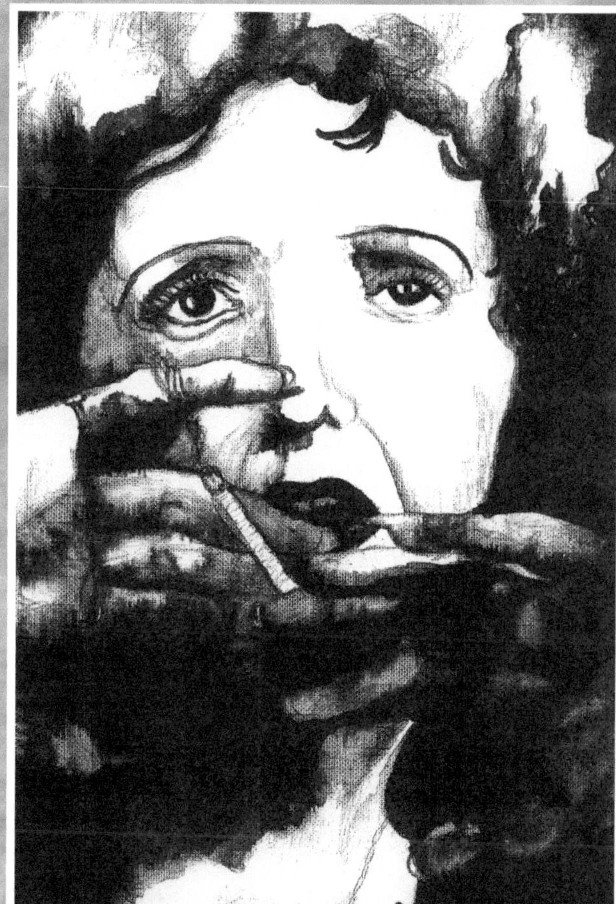

Come September, come November,
Lotte sing of Anna
And Anna of Weill
Awhile to catch
This blaze of leaves
The stoplight turns red,
As scarlet as your lips,
Your cigarette's tip,
Whatever few precious days
Left to our season.
Time passes golden
And silver petals
Down the street.
Up blooms the night,
A Pirate Jenny
Dreams at last fulfilled.
Come ship pulled by the moon.
Come freighter of music
Out here in the stars.
We are lost like lamps
Among such strange boulevards,
But love is a guidepost
And every legacy a lady
In the dark there, singing.

21

Winter, strange weather,
The london bridge
Is coming down
Across the channel
Like a lover
And Marianne is the torch,
The cabaret keeper,
Keeper of the flames.
Smoke and put on perfume.
Smoke and walk in this room,
Modern moderator of excess,
Fearless survivor of fear
Preserving life
Blue with the mist
Of a cosmos lined up,
A cosmos painted up
Through the sky lights
Of this stage.
Smoke rings well,
And water ripple,
The madonna blue heavens
Neither virgin saint
Nor whore sacred,
The madonna midnight blue
Heavens only tender and more tender
Where our angels all smoke
And hum blue lullabies as prayers

Dawn, Holly go,
Holly step lightly
As ivy, as Ginger
Without Fred Astaire.
In your eyes
Smoke did get,
But where there's mascara,
Where there's victrolas,
Where there are ash trays,
Why worry about tears?
"Cry more, pee less,"
Grandma once said,
Wiser than all
The pearls of Tiffany's,
Bright and seeing clearly
As all the windows
At Chartres

Victor

"Heroines Unlikely"
Poem & Art
by Stephen Mead

"Heroines Unlikely"
is dedicated to my
Mother, Marie,
& my Sister,
Marianne, with love.

Girl, eyes as buttons,
cornflower blue,
hair, the
tassel silk...
What you know
is instilled wonderment.
What you experience
will be innocence
Until it is wise.

2

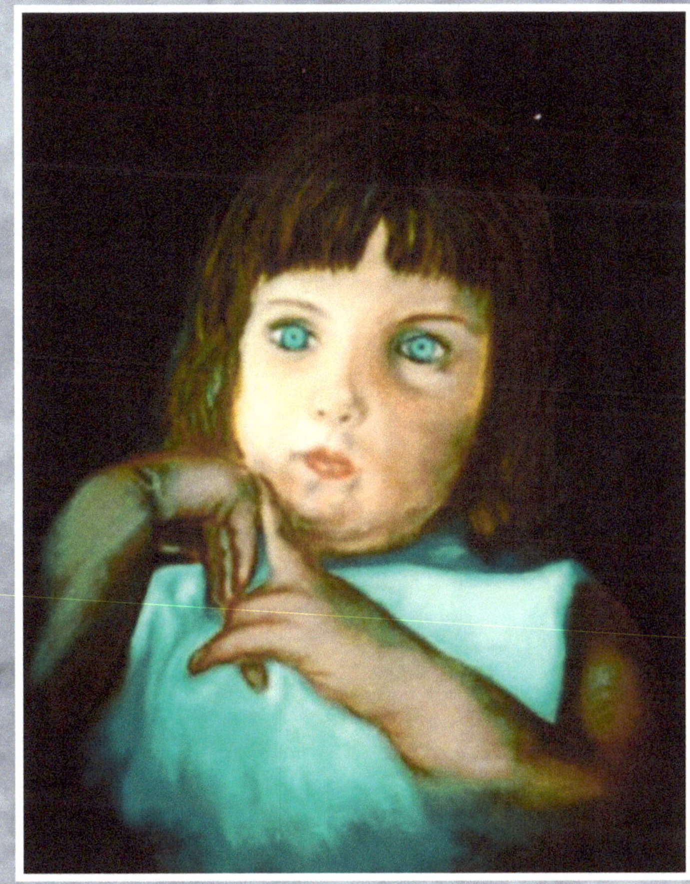

Comfort, the mother
stands for, strength
in the
mouse-brown,
Meek and myopic,
so the child
may be sure
Of the steady hold,
the seeing gaze

4

Soldier of light,
with flaming eyes,
Waiting and wading
Through the orphans
of wars
Now gripping
To the tired lifeboat,
Your shoulders of hope,
A camouflage dock
Riding storms out.

6

Daphne a swirl,
the bark spirals,
The sprigs with stars
Glittering
in your sagacious
watch,
Earth mother warrior
swearing,
"True, you have felled
many,
but none shall have
this one,
this owl eye outflying
the arrow's mark.

8

Pallors of fathoms,
blackness of waves,
This shawl is a net
of fish secrets,
The brine, a tonic
to drink.
Sand ageless,
and swimming...

She is all that explores.

10

Dream maid
in the sea of Mer,
Where colours run
Your senses flow
In the REM beats,
The breathing,
a sigh melody...
Hear the spirit travel
Nap after nap,
And night by night.

12

She is the soul
of many,
The novelist
to her novel,
Poet to her poem,
Unowned
but dispensing
Gifts of rhyme
and images,
The eyes of insight
Through which to see
The versions
we may name,
Though it is her voice,
Her story, becoming.

14

From such voyages
can come
Such revelry true,
the nuns of flight
Off the bravest
fool's ship,
Holding their key,
these cigs,
Mooring on the rock
of God,
The sea of Mary.

16

Translucence,
transcendence,
The legs still kicking
Cotton puff clouds,
The windy vistas,
The memory hills
For future histories
Made scriptless
as air,
The kindest
passion play.

18

Mercy too,
the statues
turned flesh,
Consoling
the goddesses,
Frail and mortal,
From movies
Ridicule envies
The voluptuousness of,
Or identifying, seeking
To escape through,
saved,
By screened vestibules
When it is raining
in the dark
Outside.

News reels peal
Bells in the visuals,
These corteges
of mourning
We become
one through,
Sailors in the sailing
Through assassins,
plentiful,
And personalized
politics

Ask Mrs. Ethel,
Casualty or con
in the cause,
The mystery,
roses, sweet,
Magnify the thorns of
When the dove of love
Passed through
the torturous,
The frying scapegoat,
Heretic of time.
Generations pass.
Does any answer come
Gentling
the questioning?

24

Hiro, Nagasaki,
What of your travesty,
Your saga of silk
as skin
Kimonos,
the patterns ablaze?

26

Heroines, unlikely,
come
From such turf,
The territory of faith,
The fortunes of destiny
Dreaming,
"choose me",
Or be surely
circumstance
Pure with this vision,
Despite victimization,
To dream, be, fly.

28

Fruit of the vine,
lady day blossoming,
Lavender magnolia,
ruby amethyst,
Of soft purring song
And horns of pain,
Our Gabriel,
blessed be,
The child
who got plenty.

30

Music is the world,
This shell to your ear,
The guitar strings,
veins.
Nothing travels
like acoustics,
Landscapes of legs,
Nike-winged.

32

Sidekick, swim,
stroke by stroke,
Chin not always
just above,
But the eyes,
Steady
on the current,
Sun-fluxing,
Virginia's surf...

34

It is adventure all,
This torch
sheds light on,
This liberty lamp
freeing
The ideas
if not the beings,
The needs
if not the links.

36

It is adventure all,
This gospel of truth
Sojourners share
'round traditional
fires of bravery.

"From The Sea Of Myths"
poem and
by
artwork
Stephen
Mead

...for the times when we need to be
our own heroes or heroines
and for the times
we need reminders of them...

From between Imbros and Tenedos
Where fogs roll away
And the spray is kissed by pink
And the rocks shimmer bronze
And waves break galloping,
The summoned myths
Begin to approach,
Gods and Goddesses
At this diaphanous gate,
This portal of timelessness
Infinite in chimera,
The ephemera of eons
Blowing substance through our lives

2

Watchman, whom so ever goes
Through here
Must know the code
For the blue heart's riddle,
The amulet of the stained glass staff
Offering safe passage
To the noble and the lonely
Waking past our guardian's mask
In his knowing coyote gaze

4

Shelter, shelter,
This is the solace whispering
Persophone back to Demeter,
The maternal robes
Cloaking innocence as sage
In a hood of red riding,
In palms pressed against the window
Of glass life,
Of strength in fragility
For all mothers, all daughters
Learning to be sisters
Beyond susurrus wars
And the storms of birth pangs

6

Bespeak, the annunciation foretold,
The testament of ancient prophesy,
Eye to eye
Communicating
By sight and silence,
The secrecy of flames
Air returns to
Mothlike,
Feeding the wick,
The sweat of wax
Still rosary- beading

8

Hina, come to us.
Hear the shell song.
Descend in our glade,
Moon silver, water fall
Foamed, delightable light,
Ebullient and jubilant
With the tidal pulsing
Evergreen

Helen and Salome, the dancer
And the dance turns to your allegory,
Twin movement through lies,
Those man made
Of the wily and feminine
True only to her tale,
Unwritten,
Not the heresy, not the crimes
As shame
Like veils
Sheds its skins,
Snake in the garden,
Essential to fertility

Mermaids, I have heard,
The drowned incarnate
Regathering through streams,
The eyes of gills, the algae
Gloss, the pearl sheen pure
In the will o' the wisp music,
And tresses dancing
And fingers beating
To the currents pulse
Galleons gleam in
Naming our treasures,
So many measures
Of sandy light
To which not even the dumb
Are blind

Thetis and Amphitrite
Rise, ignite
Seal splendor, dolphin glee,
The fins of infinite
Holding the harp strings
As scales of surf
To be played wide
As all oceans can reach
The shores of
Mother Earth, Father Sky

16

Saturnalia, satyr saturn
Named, you bring wings
To the heavens, your span,
A parade, and joyful,   the noise
Trumpeting, gourd-funneled,
The breath of mistrals,
Minstrels, tsunamis
Celestial as meteorites
In flight.
Beardful of stars,
Hooves, the shine of brine,
We are yours for the summoning,
Come, stroke us as shuttlecocks,
And send us, orgiastic,
Showering comet tail rockets
For the promise of more
Glowing in the aftermath
Of heights Arcadian

Diana, Diamanda,
Siren of owls, ravens and bats,
Banshee of beasts
Targeting Lilith faith.
Fly Ariel messenger,
Dearest priestess of electricity
With volts in your hair,
Lightning from your eyes------
Yes, fly, re-righting
The wrongs of the sanctimonious,
Goddess swords the scythes
In your veins, your voice

So Endymion wakes, spell broken,
To the chariot of Hecate,
The driven bull, the passionate trail
'deliverance from mine enemies',
is surely the gospel through
by the vows of these woods,
the good and the true,
nebulae rushing with winds
Hecate, evanescent,
Blankets with her presence
To hold the promise of reunion
As opal of twilight, as lamp
Of the moon

Cronus is meanwhile
Metaphor of the dethroned,
Beached on survival,
Brooding over it all.
Massive the shoulders,
The mane, the manacles
Of mansions gone to dust
Junks ferry the efforts of,
The kingdoms, the kings,
Freer in oceans
Ruled only by gypsy empresses

24

Lament, la mer, an Appollonian
Laocoon this, of the adrift
Castaways, Poseiden, Hades, Zeus,
Lambent and lucent
With the lessons of regret
Which their own threats
Became the serpeants of,
Barnacled lode stones,
Lagan lodestars of the froth
Circumstance depicts
The tragedy of, vortex fixed
For all time, unless,
Man saves
Man saves
Man saves

26

Thus Eurydice caught by Pluto
Tried to teach Orpheus
But Orpheus looked back,
Taught, as are we all,
To project, to reflect
And give such feelings to the lyre,
Make the instrument itself become love
To pull us, our very beloveds,
From the hells, from the darknesses,
So why should returning
Be such punishment?

28

Half angel, half eagle, Yemana
Might ask this, Santerian goddess
Of rain, of womb balance, nurturing
Harmony,   the union between poles
Our souls are the magnets of,
On guard amid chaos,
One eye, Yemana's, one eye
The talons which will clutch,
Consume any enemy
Who may see us as prey

30

Epona, too, is such a protectress,
Celtic and kind for all horses wild,
All stallions and mares,
All pony colts running
From the shadows of ropes,
The bits of slavery,
Emerald-grey in her watchfulness,
The vigilance, equine,
For lunar guidance,
The harbors of night

32

Set down your swords, your helmets,
Kwan Yin is coming.
Shower your petals.
Shield every bird.
Hand come to hand,
Not in combat,
But grace,
For Kwan Yin is Mary,
Endless mercy, Kwan Yin
Is compassion, ruth to our sores,
The scars of wars,
And we are at peace
With the truce
Of healing

34

Down past chasms, fissures,
The fossilized carcasses of ships,
The jettisoned cargo coral takes,
Aphrodite shuts her eyes,
Humming to the samsien
Of bubbles and fins,
The valentine pearls ascending,
And, titanic, the romance,
The ghostly lulling
Of mesmerism.
Sleep, dream, shell awash
In the rhythm, breathing liquid,
You will find your way

36

From trees we became
Surely as legendary
As fairy stories and fables,
Our arms home to cats,
And as lambs to lions,
Birds as well, sharing
The embrace
From such glittering black,
The bark warm wilderness,
This reverie forest, love,
Between our noses,
And out of our childhoods,
The tales, the histories,
One hundred and one nights
Of centuries realized between
Then and tonight

In our eyes

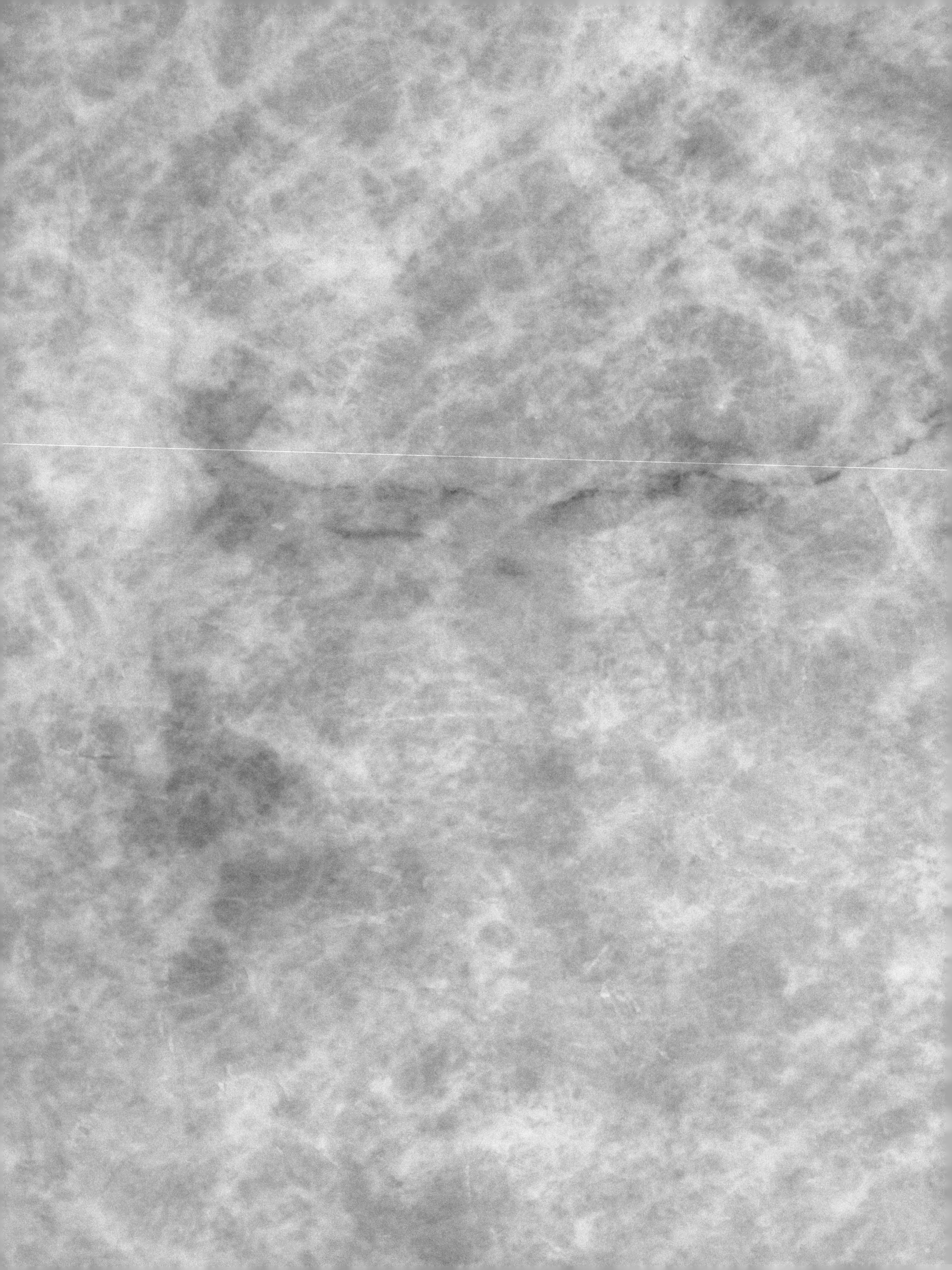

"We
Are

More Than
Our Wounds"
poem and art
by
Stephen Mead

29

"We Are More Than Our Wounds"

by

Stephen Mead

(This book is dedicated to David DeNoble)

Originally published by
NewAgeDimensions June 2004

copyright2006 StephenMeadArt

Here, at the center, left

ventricle to aorta right,

the scars are pure

from the efforts of work,

the moment by moment

bleeding to heal.

Hear the murmur

and more bass drums

deeper, slower,

with a lover's head

against that prayer.

2

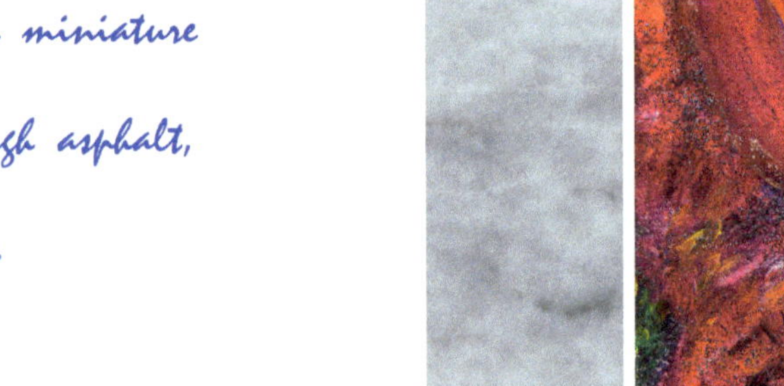

Listen, we know so many

of us have the flaws

of small cracks,

but perhaps it is perfection

nevertheless

as a wilderness in miniature

might spring through asphalt,

gentling the coarse.

4

Yes, I feel the geyser of that

and the bridge when we pass,

familial of the blood

and of the fear,

crossing our hearts,

laying our hearts

across each other,

a sacred cross.

6

Now in the cross that we share

there is a little Wounded Knee.

Its links tell of the feather dancer,

sacred and fancy,

and of an earth ceremonious

to feed the worship of.

How many spilled drops

are pooling still?

How much an ocean

of thundering bison?

Ah, from the prairies

resurrections of echoes come:

tom toms to the well of heavens

but with no rifle

nor tomahawk in hand

as the feet beat

again amen

in the ghost dance of stars.

Kneel down here.

Feel this pearl of energy

these fingers cup.

It swirls as music

from organs which pump

the veins back to breath.

Catch,

and up arms

travels the hum

of you now kneeling,

becoming safe

right in your own heart.

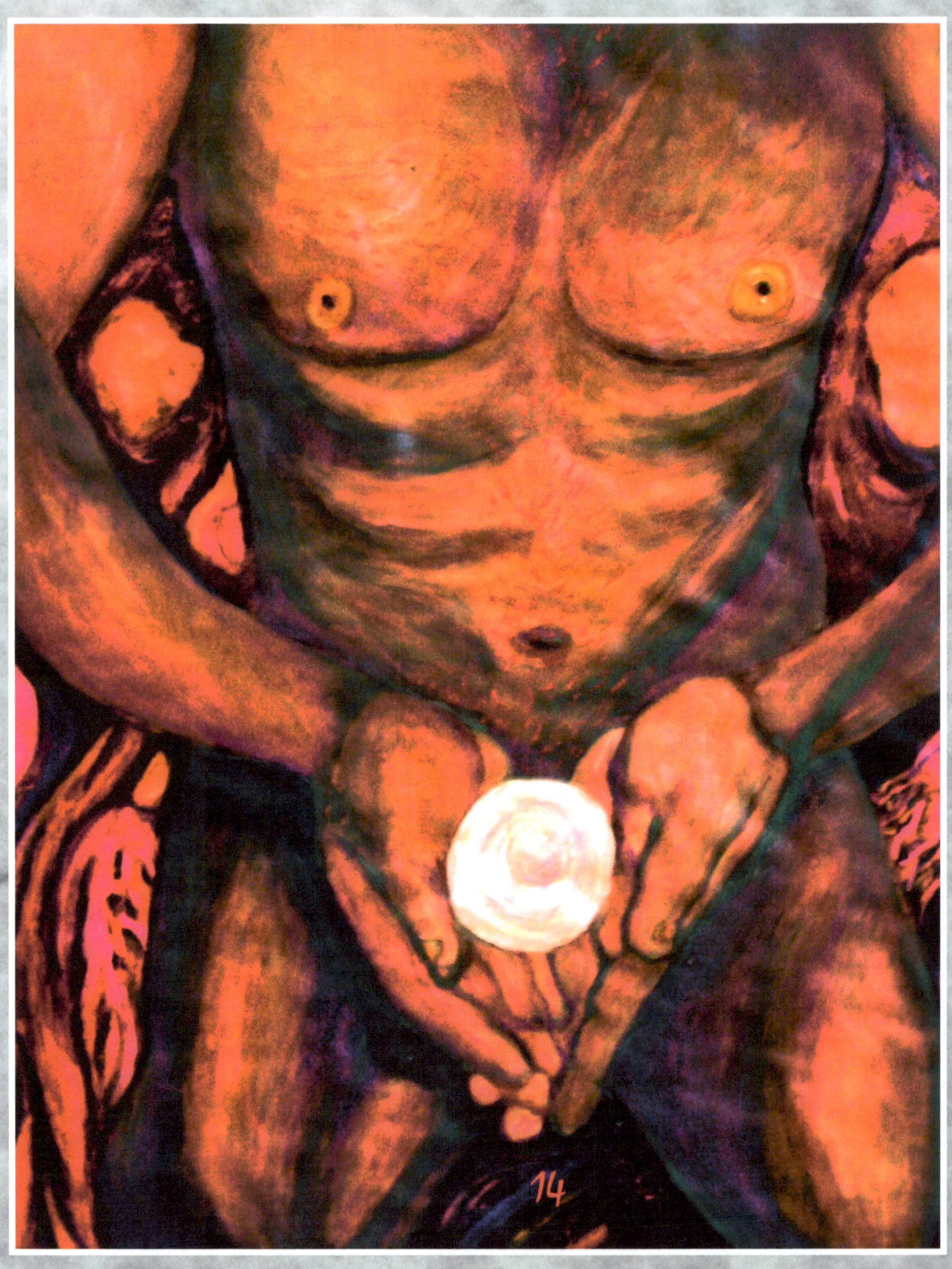
14

Raise it golden then,

a crystal orb,

a chalice of sun,

and one slender red thread

with bells of annunciation

in reverie for the coming one.

Saints hands

fold over as wings

redder with what's up

the sleeves

now gloriously open

to the love ever present

and for so long ignored.

Yes, look inside this heart.

See the Mandala

which can't be denied.

It has the patterns of tile

for all the floors ever paced,

and the marks of glass stains

for whatever pain makes belief.

18

Hips too tremble with this,

the pelvic, the pubic,

blooming lilies

with tender pistils,

and are we not

flowers of bone

sea fed from the marrow,

our mother's first uterus

that tide in us still?

21

Now take this trowel.

Excavate right here

the mines beneath the levels

fathoms under

the known landscapes

of hurt,

and the forgotten sands,

and the surf churning

jewels back to beaches

glinting with expeditions

of the oldest

archeological souls.

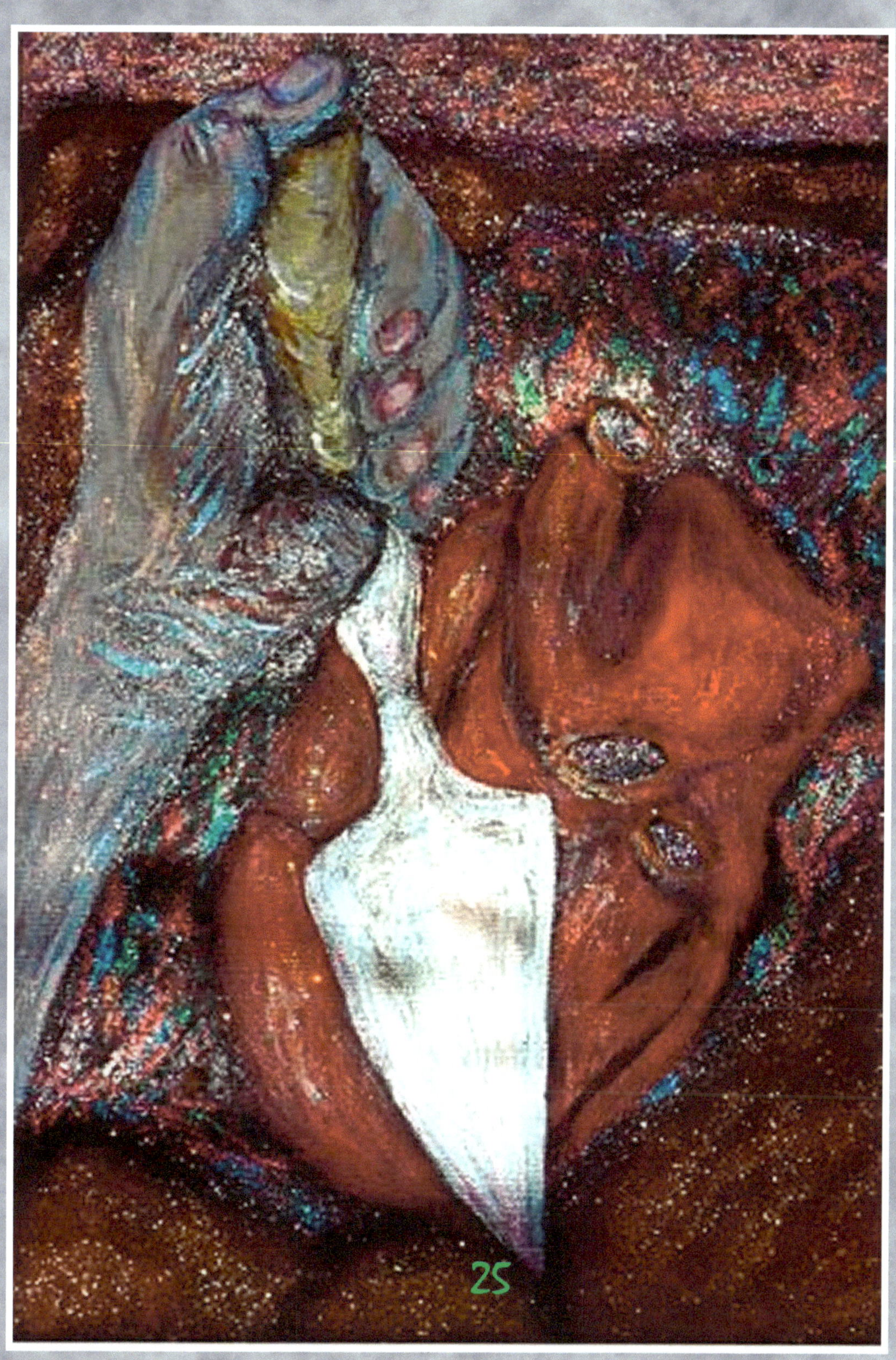

Surely if you make a tourniquet
of your heart
it is on its own
an unnamed Turin Shroud.
Call it familiar.
Pet and pat it, blessing up,
smiling down
on the bandages which swaddle
what very nearly burst
now grafted back,
stitched for the road.

26

27

29

This is the steeple again
and the valentine two shapes
may weave
a sound shawl from
through legacies ancient
making a new temple
until the bodies are at home.

28

Still there will
be struggle's knot:
the chains to wrestle,
the oppositions which lock.
Can we turn them to ivy
and the garlands
of Christmas lights?

Can we turn in tandem
from the sport and the hunt
not as Romans
or Trojans
but only as humans at last
not on the run?

Yes from the rubble
of a hundred and one broken
climbs not a God
but one who's simply questioned,
and there is not the Goddess
looking on,
but the one who's only listened,
the eyes vigilant antennae,
the lips Trillium's reassurance.
Come on. Come, you can
that silence has sung.

This then is the finale
ad in fin.
This then is true Hoa Binh,
making peace that is,
peace in another language.
But we are all born with tongues
and as instruments of impermanence,
so let us make use of
what grains we have,
drawing maps in the cosmos,
little lay away plans
for our descendants
to live loving
one another for once
and for always
the best ways they can.

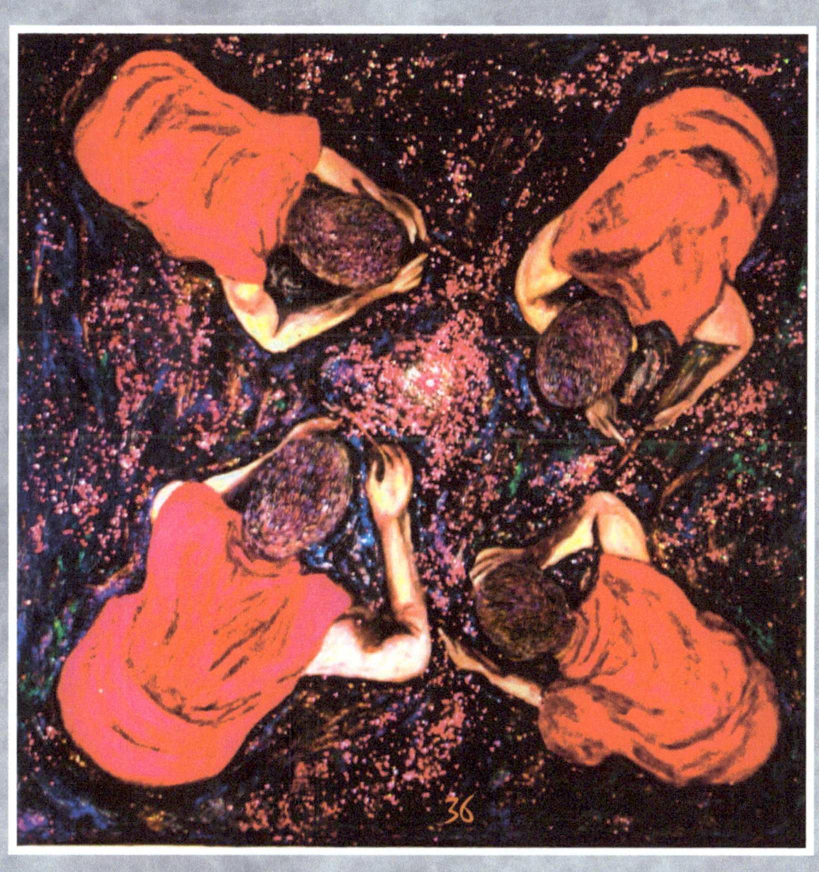

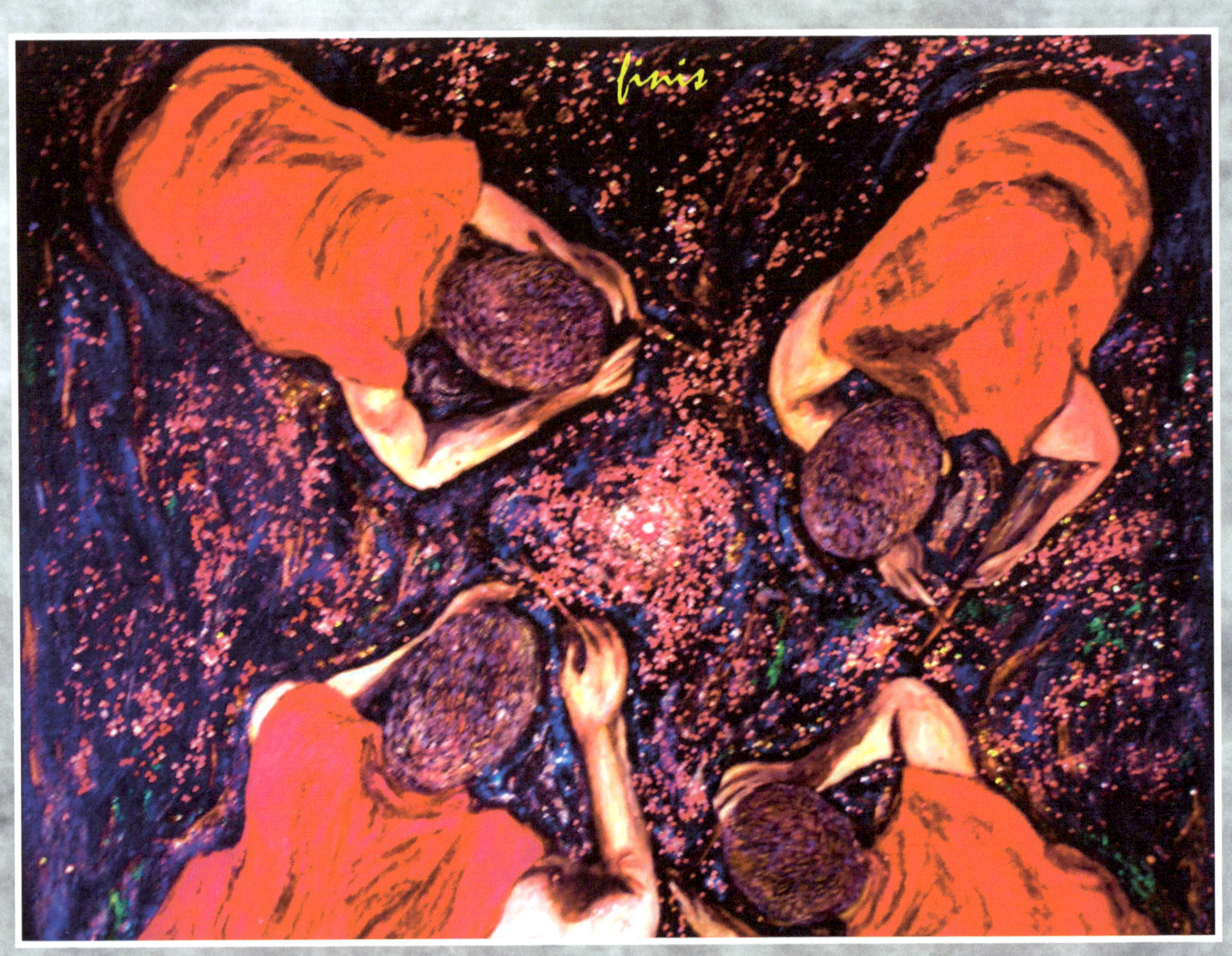
finis

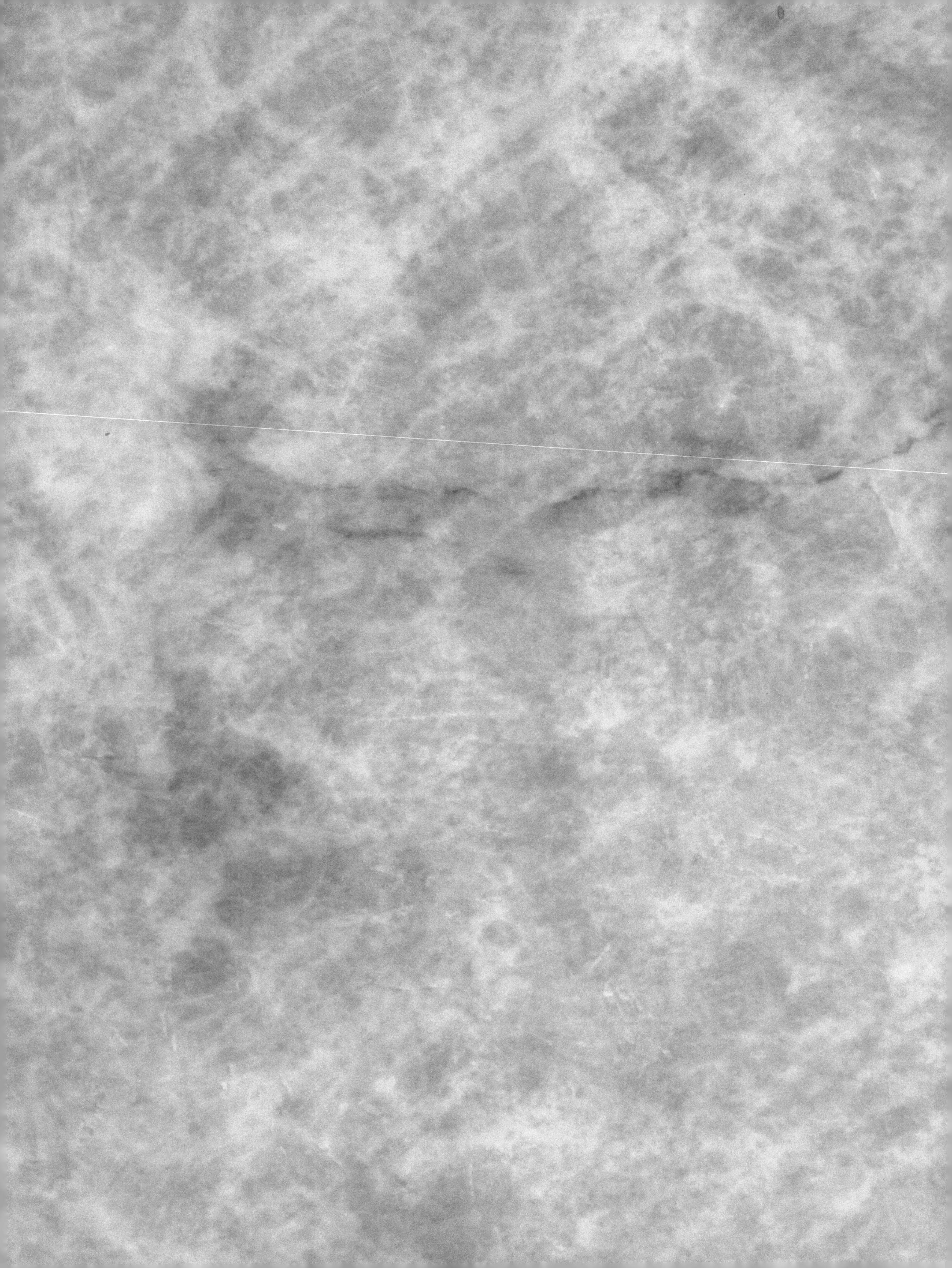

thank you

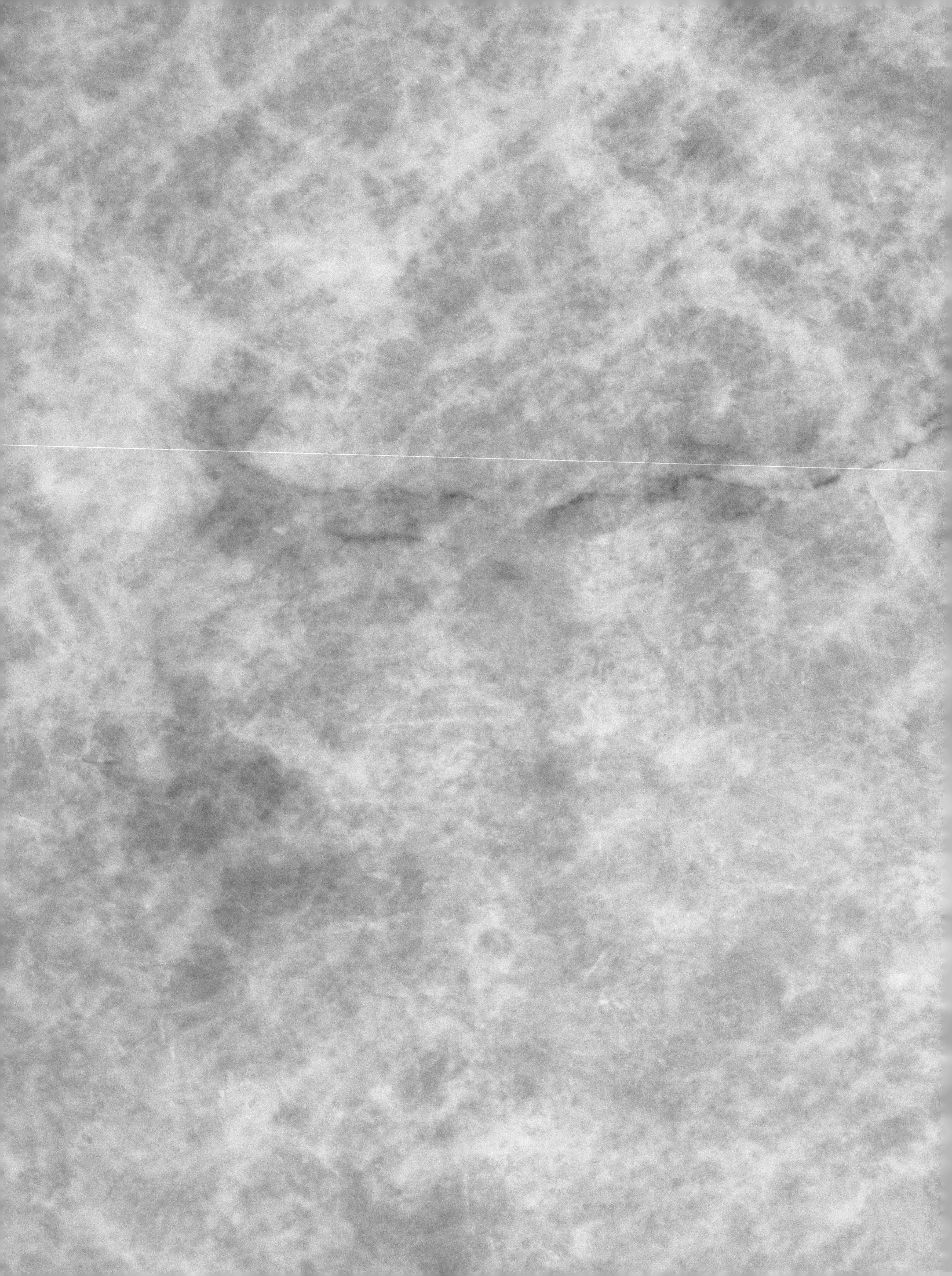

Stephen Mead is a
writer and artist
living in the northeast
of New York State.

Google his name
for links to other
art and writing
he's done.